AS THE

MOONLIGHT

SHINES

As The Moonlight Shines, 2nd Edition
ISBN: 978-1-68454-247-5

Printed in the United States of America.

Cover artwork by Jorge Santiago, Jr.
Book design by Jorge Santiago, Jr. and Nick Ulanowski
Watercolor illustration on page 29 by Kristin Palmer
Photographs on pages 61 and 67 by Nick Ulanowski
Illustration on page 79 by Jorge Santiago, Jr

10 9 8 7 6 5 4 3 2 1

AS THE
MOONLIGHT
SHINES

Nick Ulanowski

Forward

*"I've seen broken hearts like broken dreams,
like broken bodies under the pale street lights tonight"*
--Blood for Blood, 2004, Victory Records

After my lifelong friend was stabbed to death while selling drugs, I didn't know to handle it. I was 19 years old and so was my deceased friend. I didn't understand the world's response to the tragedy. I had survivors guilt. I felt great loss and pain. The world was a dark and seemingly hopeless place. Listening to music and writing poetry were my only escapes from these cruel realities. Writing poetry was my way to cope and maintain any semblance of hope. Poetry was how I organized my thoughts. I wrote to discover what I thought and how I felt. Writing poetry helped me figure out the world.

In 2009, I collected many of the poems I had written over the years and I self-published them in a book titled As the Moonlight Shines. This is a second edition of that book. In many ways, As the Moonlight Shines represents and reflects a different chapter of my life. The book's title poem asks the question, *"Will I live to see myself at age 25?"* Spoiler alert: I did. Today, I'm in my early thirties. And I'm still alive and kicking. My heart's still beating, and my lung are still pumping. I fucking made it! How about that?

The truth of the matter is that I no longer struggle with many of the feelings I was writing about in this book. I have a different lifestyle. And I no longer feel the same lack of direction in life. My daily feelings of loss are no more. My brother Johnathan Fields isn't forgotten but my grief didn't forever remain. I've moved on. I've grown. I'm not the same man I was ten years ago. Nevertheless, this book is a piece of my soul. It represents and reflects a past creative endeavor that I can't escape from. I wouldn't be the same person today without As the Moonlight Shines. For this reason, this is a book that means a lot to me and it's worth revisiting. However, when printing a second edition, it did need some revisions and additions.

Two of the poems from the first edition have been omitted. I omitted "Quite A Bit" because I was too uncomfortable with the fact that it could be interpreted as glorifying gang violence. With a little bit of hesitation, I omitted "Four Letter Words" because today I have a fundamental disagreement with some of its philosophical message. Considering some of the other content I gleefully chose not to remove, this reasoning might not make sense to readers who are familiar with the book's first edition. But oh well. I'm the author and it was my decision.

Despite the omission of these two poems, there is considerably more content here. The first edition of As the Moonlight Shines contained 82 poems. This second edition contains 94 poems. With the two omissions, this means there are 14 new poems in this edition: "Fuck It All," "A Man Named Dan." "Under the Night Sky Alone," "Nighttime Coffee," "Someday, Some Way," "Blackness," "The Next Destination," Skull Crack," "Just Do It, Sex Sells," "Like Hounds in a Pack," "Better Than Suicide," "Sex, Drugs, Power and Murder," "Hazy Fire," and "Poets Are Assholes". In addition to these new poems, there's brand-new cover art from the brilliant comic book artist Jorge Santiago and two interior illustrations from Jorge Santiago and my friend Kristin Palmer. I couldn't be more pleased with how this second edition turned out.

So, come with me, folks. I hope you enjoy the journey into the deep, dark depths of my mind. The poems in this book tell tales of loss, regret, sorrow, anger, pain, death, destruction and darkness. However, this is also a book about how to cope and find hope. In spite of it all, I hope you can see that, dear reader. Because even under a starless sky on an empty road, there is always the light of the moon to guide your way.

Nicholas Ulanowski
Chicago, Illinois
November 28th, 2018

Table of Contents

(Includes a watercolor illustration by Kristin Palmer)

(Includes a photograph by Nick Ulanowski)

(Includes a photograph by Nick Ulanowski)

(Includes an illustration by Jorge Santiago)

I Fear Nothing

I fear nothing, it's my greatest fear
And yet nothing fascinates me, it fascinates me to no end
The idea of nothing inside, just a meaningless existence
With nothing to see and with nothing to be
Nothing but chaos and unconscious nihilism
It truly is my greatest fear.. Nothing, absolutely nothing

As the Moonlight Shines

What is it you see when you look up at the night sky?
Do the tears fall out of sorrow or anger at the lies?
What is it you see in the waves that crash into the shore?
Do you wonder of a time when less was more?
Do you know that in your heart I still can be here?
As you crack open your beer, is it because death is near?
Where do you pain, have you no sense of gain?
Is it because the cold has overtaken what once kept you sane?
Why are you sitting there on this dock?
As your sobs thicken you toss into the distance a single pebble, a rock
When it drops into the lake, do you regret past mistakes?
Is it really too late, with doom and gloom as your inevitable fate?
How do you survive without what you had always relied?
Will you rise up from the ashes of demise?
The tears in your eyes as you again gaze up at the night sky
Will they even mean shit to any passerby's?

I can't believe I'm alive, I can't believe I survive
Will I live to see myself at age twenty-five?
As my watch reaches midnight I am consumed by the lies
And the only remaining answers wash over me as the moonlight shines
I can't believe I survive, I can't believe I'm alive

Who are you calling out to as you begin to scream and shout?
What is this about, your growing sense of all-encompassing doubt?
And why are you cursing the whole damned human race?
Is it because your heart was broken and it left a fatalistic aftertaste?
Was it a just from a failed 'chase' of a girl, or something else?
An old friend who abandoned you, you scream, is this why in the sun your eyes melt?
Or is it merely a product of your current fast life on the run?
And do you really find comfort in your concealed gun?
As the shouting stops, why do you go right back to your beer?

Does it help you forget that it seems like she's no longer here?
Or does it maybe numb the pain of my departure?
Is that why you have sought the legacy of an iconic martyr?
As you pass out on this dock, did it make anything better?
Would in the morning you even remember you had written her a letter?
As the wind blows the double-sided pages into the lake
With everything to lose, how is it you perceive you have nothing at stake?

I can't believe I'm alive, I can't believe I survive
Will I live to see myself at age twenty-five?
As my watch reaches midnight I am consumed by the lies
And the only remaining answers wash over me as the moonlight shines
I can't believe I survive, I can't believe I'm alive

When all hope has vanished, you look up to the night sky
And the light of the moon is the only presence, you say, understanding your cry
When you don't have a prayer you look up to the night sky
As the stars glisten you scream for lost times
But you know you're alive as the moonlight shines…

Lunar Eclipse

I sit in my black Chevy on the side of the road
Windows rolled down, and the air is cold
But the moon is warm as its light shines down
Its glow falls over both me and the prairie
As it slowly, slowly, fades into oblivion

Marilyn Manson is playing softly
Coming from the stereo of my car
As the smoke from my cigarette
It rises, and fully yet partially covers
The illuminating moon
That is until, it once again… disappears

I lie back and sink further into the cushion of my seat

Moonlight Daze

No stars in the sky, only the moon
As I'm driving home in my Chevy, resisting the swoon
Its light shines down upon me and casts an intoxicating spell

Into my eyes, this light enters, but there is no fright entailed
It washes over my essence with the short-term memories of tonight
It's very rare that I say this, but for now, 'all is right'

In the Eyes of The Damned

There are no limits in the eyes of the damned
You are but a dream in the eyes of the damned
We're all here to just be exterminated in the eyes of the damned
Because humanity is like a pest problem in the eyes of the damned

Only when a man has lost everything is he free to do anything
Only when a soul abandons hope can they free themselves of pain
Free themselves of fear like seeing not a thunderstorm but gentle rain
Lose the ability to love and free themselves from ecstasy
Lose all traces of humanity and free themselves from vanity

Do you dare take a look into the eyes of the damned?
Do you dare look at the misery, the hopelessness and the despair?
A future wasteland of a planet can be seen in their misanthropic glare

A civilization that will one day come crashing hard down to the ground
Along with all of its socialized morals, one-way systems and false ideals
Some may fall to their knees and pray to a higher power
Others may even see it as the great return of their savior and martyr
But we all did it to ourselves, in fact we were doomed right from the start
And in the eyes of the damned there will be no surprise or even resistance
as the entire fabric falls apart..

There is no point in the eyes of the damned
Our only purpose is to survive in the eyes of the damned
Nothing is everything and everything is nothing
Do you dare take a look into the eyes of the damned?

Funeral for My Sanity

Welcome to the funeral
Remove your cap and bow your head
for this sorrowful day of mourning
And for our tremendous loss
It's such a tragic loss
Especially for me,

'cause it's the funeral for my sanity

I hope you enjoy the ride
as you step into the endlessness of time
And take this ill-considered journey
Through the dark and twisted tunnels of my mind
Past the brick walls once paved in gold
but now covered, in flies, disease and mold
And through the space that's in between them
that will feel so sickly and cold
A world that once shined brighter than the sun or moon
but now a color-consuming vacuum

This funeral for my sanity
is not held at a church or synagogue
There's no prayer or other mumbo jumbo
or any romanticism of the past
There's no kind words of remembrance
of all the heartfelt times that couldn't last
There's no preacher man or music
or any talk of leftover essence
And the pain that is being immensely felt
is the ripping of a once balanced equilibrium

Just know that in this pit of hell
Any hopes or dreams you may once have had
will vanish faster than a raver's heart attack
And as time will then tell
They aren't ever coming back

A Hermit Woodsman's Ingenious Plan

The lacked constriction of these eyes has brought upon them perpetual incineration
Yet it has simultaneously sanctioned this eruption, as my third, expands in dilation
From deep inside I break free, and release, these words to be so direly spoken
They roll off the tongue, no remorse, as I stare intensely into the campfire
As the paining light burns into my soul these relentless passions of desire

"Virtue is its own reward, and to have a reward you must first achieve
And to socially achieve means no one will ever just up and leave
This plan I have in store will bring upon this world more virtue and reward
And destruction, mayhem and gore as a universally holistic chore
It shall be accomplished not to impress or please, but for the bribery

As the path to such achievement is all I need for any glee
And I never gave a rats ass about any harmonious state of humanity
Merely a serum to whip out this parasite spreading faster than cut-down trees
And faster than the freezing cold winter that is killing off the bees"

Forehead dripping perspiration as I lean back into my seat
I whip my sweat now knowing exactly how I am to carry out this feat
And the ensued outcome I have in store of catalytic inspire
It will be its own reward, this phenomenally ingenious conspire
Yes it shall, I think to myself, as I glare harder into the fire
All will tremble in my wrath, it's really quite simple math
But I must first carry out the methodology of which I have in store
But as for right this second I am to wait, before its worldly engorge
The antidote should arrive tomorrow which is when I must cut the blue wire
Dismantle the clock and phone and then jack from a car three tires...

Alive with Dark Eyes

A blank stare of terror embracing the night air
And an expression of worth in a beastly lair
It's the cope of the earth and the fire of lurk
As I'm swimming in murk and blazing my irk

(I can't believe I survive, I can't believe I'm alive
In a world of enterprise in which I plot the demise
Longing re-design and a lacking fear of disguise
Will I live to see a time I'm not crying inside
I can't believe I'm alive, I can't believe I survive)

Bright lie, Dark eye, Scam try, Deny
Bright lie, Dark eye, Scam try, Deny
Bright lie, Dark eye, Scam try, Deny

(I can't believe I'm alive, I can't believe I survive
Will I live to see a time I'm not crying inside
Longing re-design and a lacking fear of disguise
In a world of enterprise in which I plot the demise
I can't believe I survive, I can't believe I'm alive)

The glare and blank stare is fading from wear
Entangled in a forest you would read in my eyes
There's no room in my eyes for crooked schemes or sunrise
Alive to survive, Survive for the ride

Uptown Urchin

Turned the corner
Shit all seemed well and good
But I know now in the end
That I would've should've could
Late in the afternoon
With nightfall about to come
Puffing on a cinnamon clove

Sundown
See the motherfucker scram
Is it just a dream?
More like a nightmare so obscene
Or a calling I had to follow
Yeah, it's pretty hard to swallow
Slangin' herb ain't what I want
But I can't stop

Stab 'em quick
Before any screams are heard
Helpless like a bitch
Take it in the stomach
And two more in your arm
Leave the body out in the open
Not our concern

Gunned the gas
Couple coppers on my ass
Nowhere to hide or turn
Knew those days would never last
But concluded like a bang
Of an M-80 in the night
With the playa I drove to meet
Nowhere in sight

Reminisce
Forgotten in the mist
And releasing from your wrist
But it's worthless like the tested piss
Dead homie I'll always miss
Not a day goes by that I don't wish
I could've said it

Just a Poem I Wrote

Misery loves company and I'm so goddamn alone
I have no one to share it with, so far away from home
Reveling in this misery and longing for some company
Residing in this empty darkness and feeling so unknown

Completion seems so far away and I wanna run away today
After all, when you think about it, it's all just shades of grey
Escapism can be your downfall or it can be a rise to fame and power
It just depends what goes down in the night of final hour
Like going out as a martyr in an existence so sour

You were alienated by the black dirt you had used to fill the empty spaces
And make sense of everything you had failed to notice or understand
You turned away from what could've lead you to a better, wiser path
But now it's all over in this wretched, fatal aftermath

Lost and Stranded

When you look in these eyes, what do you see?
An eternal demise or a lacking fear deep inside?
No hope for the future, it's all so far away
On the side of road, a dead engine, and my answers drift astray
All that surrounds me is old torn apart memories
As the world falls away and everyone is an enemy
Isolated and alone, just forgotten like an ancient tradition
Thoughts of despair become one with the external terror
The rear-view mirror shines towards me an image of a frowning face
A man I once knew but now never to be
What do others see? Do they see what I see?
Probably not, I suppose, with so much hidden in me
I can only dream that someday I'll have left a timeless legacy

Searching for What To Decide

Fear is replacing all of the emptiness deep inside of me
Terrified of myself and everything that others can easily see
With every decision in my life, between each option I am torn
I'm driving in the fast lane because I'd rather die than mourn
Seeing the cornfields and the prairies and everything else I'm passing
As my windows are rolled down and the tunes are turned up blasting

I drive through the middle of nowhere searching for what to decide
It's all I really need now, just to ride and ride

I look in the rear-view mirror at what I am leaving behind
The place that never valued me for my heart, my soul or mind
Without hesitation, I gun the gas and ride forward to the divine

Mental Chaos

If this state of mind was a setting,
it'd be more congested than the Dan Ryan.
With uncountable cut-short thoughts, these sparks be flyin'

I'm anxious and stressed.

Broken Road

With any luck, it'll go away
Waking up in the night in a daze
Your words are nothing more than a memory
You're just a memory I cannot forget

Feeling the caffeine surge through my system
In this dark world, I can still remember your angelic face
And in my dreams, I can still feel and taste
I wish this road could bring me back to you
And I wish my delusions would finally come true

So many broken dreams I see around me
And so many shattered images reside inside me
The cars pass me by but here I remain
I wonder where they're going
I wonder if I'm going insane

The future should look bright, but it doesn't
I reach for the stars and fall back on my ass
And it's become hard to distinguish the present from past
My mind is being held hostage like a self-imposed cage
With thoughts and emotions released out to the oblivion in a rage

Sitting on this block of cement
The cars pass me by but here I remain

I wonder where these fools are heading
I wonder if it's an aimless journey just like mine
I flick my Bic and wonder where I'm going
And if I'll ever see the day where it's my time
If I'll ever live to have my time to shine..

A Hopeless Daydreamer

This is a story of a hopeless daydreamer
He'd lie flat on his bed and stare at the ceiling
Keeping to himself, concealing his feelings
He'd sit up with his pipe all through the night
Alongside a pen and a headset, he'd feel alright

The thoughts he'd try to convey would just slip away like the sand
That would fall through the fingers of his open palms
Lost in a society of which he didn't belong

He lived in his own world, this lonely daydreamer
It was vast and tremendous, he was a legend
He had fortune and fame in this self-made world
Killas on his payroll and even had the girl

Walking alone with his eyes on the pavement
Or a menthol in his mouth, passing faces so vacant
He'd close his eyes thinking back to every false statement

Where is the line drawn between darkness and blue sky?
How easy can one live life as a paradox, between truth and lie?
How easy can it be to deny reality?
I guess the answers will only come to him in good time
Thus concludes my story of a hopeless daydreamer

Heathen Bitchboy

The day I was born it was raining outside
The day that I died was the day I broke the chains inside
But it was never good enough, never good enough for you
And I took my own life, so I wouldn't
Have to speak again to you

'Cause I'm a doobie fucker, heathen bitchboy

Yeah, a doobie fucker, heathen bitchboy
At the end of the day, I am what I am
Just a doobie fucker, heathen bitchboy

You don't know shit so don't say you do
Only a black cloud surrounding all that could be real
As I slit my throat, without any thought or feel

'Cause I'm a doobie fucker, heathen bitchboy
Yeah, a doobie fucker, heathen bitchboy
When it's all said and done, I am what I am
Just a doobie fucker, heathen bitchboy

I don't know shit so don't say I do
Only that I was never good enough
Never good enough for you

Fuck It All

I feel so helpless
Nothing's ever gonna change
I'm dying alone
I don't want to, but I will
I wish it could've been different
I didn't want it to be this way
I tried and tried
I searched and searched
Only to find.. nothing
Absolutely nothing
Just empty nothingness like the barrel
after the bullet releases into my skull

Self-Inflicted Asphyxiation

I'm a lost cause without a future whose hope has gone dry
And tonight I'm dying alone by means of this rope I begin to tie
Making the appropriate knots in all of the right places
As I think about what is to come I can almost see their faces
Their expressions of confusion as they wonder why I did it
Maybe some would even wonder if they could've made shit different
But none of that really matters because I know this is my time
After careful consideration I have decided to end this 'life' of mine

I'm doing it in my backyard under the illuminating full moon sky
I waited until this gorgeous night so I could have the perfect setting to die
I presume that they'll soon find me just hanging from this tree
With a post-it note in my pocket simply stating "have no sorrow for I am free"
No one ever asked me for anything so I was never able to give
And the one thing I myself needed... well, they never let me live
So now I'm standing on a ladder with the noose around my neck
And with a swift kick I end it all and slowly suffocate to death

Goodbye cruel world, Goodbye cruel world
If there is any 'other side,' it's where I'm headed off to
Goodbye cruel world..

Last Words

I don't know how it happened
I only know these horrid flames surround
As I make my way through the wreckage
I hear sharp crackling all around
I see your arm reach down for me
You're reaching from the floor above me
You're saying that I can make it
If I just try my hardest to grab and take it
Slowly I reach up high, I reach up towards the sky
I know I have to survive because I do not want to die

Nothing left for me to dream
Nothing left for me to be
Nothing left for me to hope
Nothing left for me to see
Nothing left for me to live
For the reaper has taken me

As my hand inches closer I almost reach your grasp
But before I manage to clutch it I hear the destruction below
I fall and fall until I land and feel a terrible blow
Laying face-up on the floor, my body is immobile
I can't even get up to stand and yet you don't understand
You shout that there's still a chance, I scream to move on and save yourself
But then I watch in horror as you're carefully jumping down to help

Nothing left for me to dream
Nothing left for me to be

Nothing left for me to hope
Nothing left for me to see
Nothing left for me to live
For the reaper has taken me

As the fumes engulf me, my whole body feels weak
My vision is getting blurry and this life is looking bleak
Like the barrel of a gun, it's all been said and done
And I give you my last words under the setting sun

I'm sorry I let you down, so sorry I let you down
These are my last words, just take them or leave them
I'm sorry I let you down, I'm sorry I let you down

Wondering to Myself

So I was wondering to myself what I should write here
On the first page of this brand new, spiffy, black, hardcover journal
I guess I'll just jot down the first thoughts that come to my mind
For better or worse, I know it'll help me unwind

It's half past seven on a Friday night
And such a dull vibe is present in this lonely setting
As I sit up in my bed, drained of my energy
Not sleeping for two days can really fuck with your synergy

I want to have a new place to call my home
I want to have published at least a few of my poems
I want a girl that would never let me let her go
I want a real paying job and I want to go back to college
And I want to move out and get out of this town

And yet I barely even seem to be getting by
Do I even try? And why wouldn't I?
I guess it's because what I don't want is to leave them behind
My mother, my friends and even my stepdad
But in spite of this fear, it seems to happen anyway
As so many in my life slowly drift away

It's a tad ironic; I think that in most of my work
I hide behind characters and concepts and literary quirks
It's rare for me to actually sit down and write how I am feeling
But instead write to escape from what I'm concealing

Next month I will be one year older
I will be turning twenty-two
Turning twenty-two
I will be turning twenty-two
And I have no clue what to do

Trapped

Aches and pains are throbbing throughout me
I don't know where to turn to make it better
Any effort for relief only worsens my surroundings
I have nowhere to hide from my own misery

(All I'll ever be is all you can clearly see..)

I'm clueless as to why I feel this way
Trapped in my own head like a rat in a cage
Any method of breaking free is beyond my comprehension
So I remain like a stray dog that is foaming at the mouth

(All I've ever been is all you could clearly see..)

Disconnected from my own condition,
I cling to delusions
because they keep me sane

A Man Named Dan

Once upon a time, there was a promising young man
He lived in the suburbs, let's call him Dan
Everyone in his neighborhood thought he was a little eccentric
His co-workers called him a whiner, his family, a dick
Dan wanted acceptance and he tried his very best
But he failed their test and he felt like a pest
On Friday nights, he never had a date
His old friends from his school days never stayed out too late
Dan watched them get married, have kids and start a career
As he worked a dead end menial job year after year

Dan felt empty inside, he felt so inadequate
As he sipped his beer at a bar and lit up a cigarette
He gazed at the pretty girls and imagined what he would say to them

He played out witty conversations in his head that he could have with them
But Dan didn't say anything, he just sat there and watched them walk out the door,
Took the last sip of his drink and asked the bartender for more
The bartender winked and she flirted but he knew that was her job
He stumbled back to his apartment, collapsed on his bed and just sobbed

Often thinking back on life's squandered opportunities
Filled with regret, various memories became blurred
It wasn't that he hated himself
It wasn't even that he hated the world
Did Dan lack the courage, the drive or the self-esteem?
His life story as he saw it read like a competitive kid who got cut from the team
"Where did I go wrong?" Dan asks as he ties up the noose
And checks to make sure the other end isn't loose
Tied to the ceiling fan like the set of a horror movie
He contemplates ending it all, making his trite life go kablooie

He was just a man, a man named Dan
Was it a self-fulfilling prophecy, never saying "I can"?
This is the story of a man named Dan
Life is challenging and scary and he always ran

Broken Light

I am broken
I serve no purpose
Not to you or anyone else
..Shattered!

I am broken
My pieces remain
In the dead and dark of the night
..Unseen!

I am broken
Just a waste of space
You can throw me out to the trash
..Worthless!

I am broken
They left me behind
Care was never given to me
..Ever!

I am broken
And I am unseen
Never to have a time to shine
..Discard!

("I was broken, shattered and unseen
But still maybe this is only a dream
Or maybe I'll know when I look to the past
Embarking on a journey that will everlast
In my death, I can see the path
In my life, I was a broken light
A broken light cast away into the night")

Under the Night Sky Alone

This road is lonely, no one is around
But I can still feel the night air as the darkness surrounds
Lost in the emptiness, am I going insane?
Where do I turn when it all looks the same?
I've lost so many in this cold hard world
From either drifting apart or it was their time to depart
Still I know she's out there (or maybe she isn't)
Out there somewhere in this world under the night sky
And maybe glancing at that very same moon and wondering "why?"

Well, if you need to find me, I've been here all along
I've been on the side of the road on the hood of my car
Next to the prairie and gazing up at each star
If you need to find me, I've been here all along
If you're out there looking, you won't go wrong

This place frees my mind as I listen to the wind
And look up at the clear sky, my reality bends
Still the loneliness consumes me, I wish she could be by my side
This thought cues a wave of sadness throughout my inside
Feeling sedated, I slowly close my eyes
And light up a cig, letting my thoughts fly
What is my purpose here? Do I even have one?
Am I cursed to wander the earth like a lone wolf on the run?
Will I ever see the day we cross paths like a rising sun?

Well, if you need to find me, I've been here all along
I've been on the side of the road on the hood of my car

Next to the prairie and gazing up at each star
If you need to find me, I've been here all along
If you're out there looking, you won't go wrong

I'm next to the prairie on West Offner Road
On the hood of my car under the night sky
If you need to find me, I've been here all along
If you're out there looking, you won't go wrong

Nighttime Coffee

When I think of you, I think of failure
I failed to keep you from leaving my side
I failed to make you want to see me again
I failed to be interesting enough for you
I failed to show you enough of a good time

It was never enough,
You said you trusted me
But it wasn't enough

I heard through the grape vine your recent news
Why couldn't you come around and give me a clue?
What the hell did I do? Did I do anything?
Or was I simply not good enough for you?

Someday, Some Way

Is it even worth trying when I fail every time?
And when the pain of each strike out leaves me feeling like I'm dying?
How do I move on? What am I supposed to do?
Just take another shot like an assclown without a clue?

Someday I will be good enough, I'll be good enough for you
But I'll no longer be around, not anywhere, it's true

I know I have other options but do I really have to act so fast?
If I relaxed and took it slow, would my opportunities just pass?
What can I do to find a way? How can I self-improve?
How do I make it past the vines to the rejuvenating blue?

Someday I will be good enough, I'll be good enough for you

But I'll be nowhere to be found, don't bother looking 'cause it's true

I'm tired of rejection, I'm tired of not getting what I want
I'm tired of lying down like a carcass left to rot
I'm tired of the loneliness and I'm tired of the mediocrity
Still I got to press forward 'cause I ain't tired enough to stop or flee

Someday I will be good enough, I'll be good enough for you
But I'll no longer be around, not anywhere, it's true

Someday I will be good enough, I'll be good enough for you
But I'll be nowhere to be found, don't bother looking 'cause it's true

Blackness

Blackness is darkness and destruction and the absence of light
Blackness is destruction and creation and the presence of all colors
Blackness is confusion as you stare up at a starless sky
Blackness is a prairie at midnight without any lightning bugs
Blackness is the disappearance of the moon and the earth
Blackness can erase misery and trauma, for what it's worth
Blackness can consume you like a moral dilemma
Blackness is beautiful in its terrifying ambiguity

Cold Winter Night Life

I see nothing clear upon this hollow shell
That resides inside of me like a wishing well
As I drop a dime through it, hoping for the chaos to end
And longing for more, I continue to endure
In this world of strife without wrong or right
It's the only harmony granted in my cold winter night life

The discontented glory of the anti-hero
A martyring endeavor, from zero to hero
If my death were to come slow then they all would know
I was afraid to depart and face that of the unknown
But if my death were to come fast like a straight up skull-bash
I would have not died in vain like thrown out trash

The darkness creeps slowly, I don't know what to do
Should I attempt escape from this hell or embrace what's anew?

I want to press forth with an axe in my hand
And conquer the impossibilities that others have damned
But with my face in the sand and a boot in my ear
I long for this suffocating nightmare to just disappear

It burns like ember way down deep in my soul
And remains suppressed, away from the cold
These memories remain no matter what road I travel
Or where life leads me or what new fights I battle
They're always here to stay and that's a-okay
Because my past is what has made me who I am today

Still what will it take for all of this sorrow to end?
Fulfillment seems so unobtainable when reality's just pretend
As I press onward, day to day.. now I lay down to rest
'Is life just a test or a vision to invest?'
I close my eyes and ask myself this once again
My head's no longer spinning as I put back down my pen

Garlic Soup for The Soul
(With an illustration from Kristin Palmer)

Do you ever wonder what it would be like
to never die as a creature of the night?
What is it that intrigues so many about this fantasy world
of undead creatures who by the living are abhorred?
They have an unquenchable thirst for blood and fright
It's human sexual desires portrayed in such a wondrous light

It was only this century their existence was officially denied
by the Catholic Church, Yet there still once was a time
it was deemed as fact by cultures everywhere across the globe
though ignorance about death and fear of the unknown
Yet today you can still see them everywhere on T.V and magazines
They're in novels and music, And countless films show these fiends

They truly don't die, and why is this so?
What is it about them that to this day still draws us in like a crow?
A crow squawking in the cemetery as the body is buried
and later dug up to find longer fingernails and hair
Then it was off to find which "house" in the village was really a lair

It was thought only to have a vampiric explanation
Yet even with modern science, the legacy lives on..

<u>Dark and Twisted</u>

What is the first thing you think of when you hear the word "darkness"?
What is the first thing you think of when one speaks of "the dark"?
For me it's the unknown and that which can't be understood
And what remains unseen to our physical eyes
I think of the abyss where who-knows-what lies

(What lies in the darkness?
Some are afraid to truly ask..)

What is the first thing you think of when you hear the word "twisted"?
And what constitutes something to be deemed in such a manner?
Well, it's right there in plain sight and maybe even shined on by a light
But there are also factors behind it we fail to understand
They're so incomprehensible that it's rendered menacing yet intriguing

(Menacing yet intriguing?
Or maybe menacing and disturbing..)

The vampyre, for instance, is a folkloric tale of the night
A symbol for purgatory who partakes in a fiendish neck bite
It's such a dark concept that one can't ever die
And is cursed to wander the earth with an immortal "life"
It's so utterly twisted when a vampyre sinks those teeth into flesh
As if been lost in the desert for weeks without rest

(Drip, Drip, Drink,
Sink, Drip, Drop..)

In my subjective perception, I see it as an addiction
While others may look rather differently at this twisted act
But still some may see nothing twisted about it, in fact

Cross my Heart and Hope to Die

I lay awake at Two A.M staring at the ceiling
Chained to restlessness as I wonder of the distant past
Memories never to be forgotten and a grief I hope not to everlast
A childhood friend who sobbed next to me on my father's deathbed
We were like brothers till the end or so we naïvely said
The last night that I saw you, I saw your newer darker path
Still I never imagined what was to come in the proceeding aftermath
Stabbed to death for cash and a couple pounds of bud
Lying on your apartment floor on a carpet now stained with blood

(I cross my heart and hope to die
This ain't a lie, it's time to die
Cross my heart and hope to die, fly away into the sky)

I fluff my pillow and close my eyes tighter than a fine-rolled joint
These questions begin to flood my mind unanswered and mingle with the rest
Why did this have to happen? Why did you have to die?
I re-open up my eyes for another failed attempt to cry,
Most people blamed the killer, I always thought it was more the slangin'
I also blamed myself for not being there to help,
And then I listened to the Christian preacher speak of a 'criminal' man
The 'criminal' he apparently meant was the one who murdered my friend
Not the atheist selling herb who died without a hand to lend

(Like a raven fly away, fly far away today
Cross your heart and hope to die
I cross my heart and say goodbye)

It's been over a year since his death and it's surreal how much I've 'grown' (?)
And to many of those around me, these changes seem to remain unknown
Will I ever get to see you again on a different plane, another time?
Or only think about you in a haze or write about you in a rhyme?
But what is this crazy life anyway? Some say it's but a dream
Some say it's just a dream but what the fuck does that even mean?
Still it really is obscene to have to die for 'green' and 'green'
My tears now begin to flow, it's somewhat strange, this smile as I weep
Maybe I can see you again tonight as I finally drift off to sleep

(Cross my heart and hope to die,
you did not depart in vain
Because I will make the world see the truth
through perseverance fueled by pain)

..Cross my heart and hope to die, I cross my heart and hope to die..

Officer

Admit you have a problem, officer
You take it up the ass
Admit you have a fault, officer
On your mother you pass gas
Admit you are a pig, officer
And have an enormous body mass
Admit you have a problem, officer
Or just continue with your wack smack-dance

The Next Destination

Rolling down this endless highway and looking out the window
The Greyhound departed from the station a half an hour ago
Night falls on the horizon, the moon is bright and full
It's the perfect time to run away from everything so cruel
I don't know where I'm going but I know there's nothing where I've been
The rumble on the concrete is graceful like the wind
The road sign says we're heading nowhere and I just don't care
The fine line has been broken from all its wear and tear

I'm tired of my job and I'm sick of my tiring life
My girlfriend left my side and my brother vanished in the night
Lying on his apartment floor next to a bloody knife
I've got nothing left to lose but I want to keep on living
It's time for me to go, it's time for me to leave
It's time that I let loose and unravel the tangled web I weave

My new destination may not be heaven on earth
I know it's still this cold hard world for what it's worth
But anywhere but here is bound to bring me happiness
Anywhere but here is bound to grant my simple wish
Somewhere on the horizon will bring me new opportunity
The world I'm leaving behind isn't good enough for me
The feeling has been mutual and tonight's the night I flee
So long and goodbye, don't shed a tear for me, don't cry
Someday I may return but tonight's the night I die

My Answers Await

I need some time to think
and get away from it all,
I wish I could have said goodbye to all of ya'll
But if I had stopped to do so, it would have made it harder
For me to leave
and be off to a far-away land,
So off and away to a new world I ran

(Where will this path take me? I don't know
But the quilt I've sewn will carry me
and soon I will grow)

Will I ever return? I cannot say

But if I do, I hope you will
at least remember my name
But either way,
I'm taking control and seizing the day

(Where will this path lead me? Where will it go?
The quilt I have sewn, it will guide me
and soon I will know)

Yes, I will soon know, and soon I will grow..

Nowhere

Dressed in all black, I walk the streets
Walking away from the end of this empty road
Not a soul is around but the darkness, it surrounds
As the clock strikes midnight in this small Illinois town

I can hear the crickets cueing the serenity
I can see the silhouettes of the trees on both sides
I can feel the moonlight as it shines down upon me
And I can see the darkened path in my mind's eye

On the other end of this road, I stop at the corner
And just wait and wait for a car to pass by
I lay down on the gravel and let the hours pass
But no one ever arrives, not a first, not a last

What am I doing here? Why did I come here?
It just seems so meaningless, it seems so pointless
I remove the headphones that were resting on my head
And then drift off to sleep as if it were my own bed

A break of sunlight, it appears up in the sky
I shoot awake and I wonder "Where the hell am I?"
Then I remember and walk back to my house
But still remain clueless as to what life's about

Skull Crack

Like a puppet, the gravity pulls me down to the ground
My head inches forward and my legs are immobile

My forehead inevitably inches towards the pavement
I can't stop this terrible collision into the cement
Our worlds have collided and I'm collateral damage
But I stand my ground in this war the best that I can
I helped battle the invaders, I never turned tail and ran
But now there will be agonizing pain as I meet my demise
I imagine there's fear in my blood-shot, wide eyes
My ears are popping like the blood vessels in my arm
The fall seems endless until my skin hits the hard ground
Like a mouse in a trap, my skull begins to crack
It opens up like a Pop Rock upon the impact
My blood remains intact as only some hits the pavement
But my brains are predominately lost like a maniac
They ooze across the concrete like a creeping turtle
Slow like a calm breeze, the pile of blood enlarges
I face the end of my journey but at least the trauma is over
I've done my part in this battle and in that, I take comfort
In this war of the worlds, I've done my part for humanity

Soylent White Society

I'm flying through the air alongside the currents of the wind
No wings, just my mind, and the physical laws that I bend
Such a perfect feeling, it was, until I gazed down at the civilization below
I had to squint both my eyes to make sense of the impending darkened glow
There was systematic movement all surrounded by thick industrial fumes
That were rising high and consuming everything under the sun and the moon
The countless ants in this world, they all wore the same homogeneous frown
As they would scurry about aimlessly, searching for a lost meaning never found
The answers I myself seek, well, they just vanished like the wind
As I then dropped to the ground, but I ain't a godsend

Petroleum and oils runs through these veins
With stocks and bonds guiding the way
When I open my eyes, what do I see?
All that could and will ever be
In this soylent white society…

I was upon their consumer-driven existence that lacked any bit of resistance
They just sulked in their self-imposed prisons while staring at an electronized screen
As each image flashed back, it would lose them in a fabricated dream
It was subliminal control, dulling their senses, and dumbing down reality
And a subtle message of conformity brought to them by the powers that be

All wrapped up as "entertainment" in what they would call "the land of the free"
A bullet hole in the brain of one of the few yet many masterminds
As I then let myself transform into all that I once despised

Petroleum and oils runs through these veins
With stocks and bonds guiding the way
When I open my eyes, what do I see?
All that could and will ever be
In this soylent white society…

The 'Line' Joke

So here I am
At the end of the line
To the much anticipated
Underground show

I pull out a pen
Bored as hell
The third line to this stanza
It looks quite well

Can I bum a smoke?
Or join the toke?
Or can you spare a line
A line of coke?

Sure, I say
You can have this line
In exchange
For your place in line

So here I still am
At the end of the line
To the apparently long awaited
D.R.I concert

A second line
I snort of coke
And write the last line
To "The Line Joke"

Just Do It, Sex Sells

Getting it on isn't pretty if you're too giddy
Or when you're a buck short on that one-fifty
Since they all said "no," you were left clueless
You went to a hooker and paid her while toothless
Through your revolting gums, you said "let's do this"
And when you put it in, you remembered "Just Do It"

There should be a minimum of sex as a gimmick
There's always a limit, regardless how you spin it
'Cause when sex gimmicks are mimicked by those who don't get it,
you told them to hit it no matter what rigged it

Oh, great Nike, how you please the consumer
And yet you spread a rumor that spreads like a tumor
Just Do It, You screw it, Nike is ruthless
Especially for people who deem themselves toothless

Like Hounds in a Pack

I take my time, adhering to all of this quiet derange
I'm about to be granted my fifteen minutes of fame
I was left behind in a world that rotted away
But if I grab this forty-five, I can seize the day
And make the pain go away, it will end as I lay
in a puddle of blood surrounded by the freaks of today

Why is it that everything seems to happen to us?
How is it they have it all, and we have barely enough?
I told all of you that we could take the power back
Us against them, like hounds in a pack

Is any of it right? Fuck that! I spite your morals tonight
Breathing the night in such a fatalistic fight
You just kick back and relax, and watch it fall to the ground
It's such a terrible sound but we know we'll soon be renowned
When we do the deed and release all our greed
It'll be a one-eighty and we'll have everything that we need
In each step taken forward towards the eternal depths of hell
The heavens forsake but we know that one quite well
At the end of the conflict: We won, we won
And they were left to experience the agony

that we had already known before this had even begun

Like hounds in a pack, we'll take all of it back
From them, from them, 'cause it's us against them
Like hounds in a pack, we'll take all of it back
From them, from them, to us what we lack

Put it Down for The Discarded

Eternal fists of rage
They lurk in the deepening dark
A pit of misery you will find
With only one light that's but a spark

Some may call it a hell
But the setting's right here on earth
Some may say it's a heaven
'Cause at least they're away from and off *our* turf

Here the discarded souls remain
Without a damn place to turn or even go
And the blood continuously spills
Even faster than the wind that'll forever flow

Eternal tears of sadness
They stream like a river from my eyes
As any call for unity amongst all people
Is reacted to only with despise

The discord, it just stays
With nothing that seems to ever change
I only wish it could..
I only wish it would..

Solitary Confinement

Nowhere to turn
When you're trapped inside
Locked in the holding cell
That's the chaos of your mind

You think of the end
Of life and of time
And the breakdown of order
Of all that is divine

Conspiracy charges
Have been leveled against you
But what can you do?
When you lack any answer
And don't have a clue

You wonder of the cataclysmic
Shattering of the glass
The shards piercing equilibrium
And how they everlast

This solitary confinement
Can be a wonderful thing
Or it can drive you insane
As to the forgotten you cling

I Should Be Dead
(Or: "Uptown Urchin, pt2")

My cell phone rang and I didn't know what to expect
Certainly not this, certainly not death
The pigs called it homicide as on the apartment floor you lied
In a puddle of blood is how it is you died
An uptown urchin had stabbed you three times as you swung
You swung your arms about, without a place to run
Another drug dealer murdered, oh, what a shame
The pigs called it a homicide as I cried out in pain
Why did you have to die on me? Why did you have to go?
How exactly that it happened, I guess we will never know
Except I do know one thing, where was I?
I could've warned you when I had the chance
Maybe then you would've changed your ways
But now instead you had to die, and in a puddle of blood you lie
Why did you have to leave? Why wasn't it ever said?
If anything, I'm the one, I'm the one
Who should be fucking dead

A Time for Rejoicing
(Or: "Uptown Urchin, pt3")

Now they finally caught the guy
He confessed it to his girlfriend and she snitched
Now it's sweet sweet vengeance upon the urchin bitch
This urchin bitch whose first name is my middle
And no that's not a riddle, I mean it completely literal
A time for rejoicing because it just may bring our loved one back
Not really, he's still dead
And I couldn't give a fuck less

Lycanthropic Endeavor

Running faster and faster through the night
Snapping my jaws on the ripped flesh I bite
Towards you I lunge, and I plunge deep into your throat
Ending your life quicker than the tightening of a rope
As I tear apart your body and begin my feast
Normally I'm a man but tonight I'm a beast
For the wolfsbane has bloomed and the moon is full
And I've dominated this human fool, establishing my rule
As the light of the moon shines down, I begin to howl
And then disappear off into the night like the shadow of an owl

(You told me I was nothing
You all told me I was nothing
No value, No worth,
Nothing special... Re-Birth!
I made a pact with the devil and I sold my soul
And under the full moon light, it's how I roll)

I wake up the next morning with a pain in my chest
And with images instantaneously flashing through my mind
What have I done? And can I put it to rest?
These images, they read of blood, gore, and ripped flesh
What the hell did I do to those victims last night?
Could I have really done *that* under the full moon light?

I get out of my bed and I roll a square
Brew some coffee and wonder of the terror
As I'm now on the porch, I notice the red stains on my clothes
I look around to see if it was spotted by any human foes

Will it ever change? Am I eternally deranged?
Is it just a chemical imbalance like a rat in a cage?
Or was it *really* the unexplainable magic of a dark mage?

(You told me I was nothing
You all told me I was nothing
No value, No worth,
Nothing special... Re-Birth!
I made a pact with the devil and I sold my soul
And under the full moon light, it's how I roll)

"You don't know what it's like to roll alone in the night
Thrashing about your jaws and taking life after life"
I was in the tent of the dark mage and was asking her 'why?'
"Prior hand to your curse, I wouldn't have even hurt a fly"
She gave me a crass smile and looked me straight in the eye
"Ahh.. But you agreed to this, so maybe *you* can answer *me* 'why?'"

I then thought back to that forsaken dying day
When all hope was lost and I thought no one would ever love me in any way
But still I had no response except "Can you just make it go away?"
"Nay," she replied, "How could I cast such a spell today?
For your hatred of humanity has but only increased,
And yet you still claim you want this uncontrollability to cease?
But if you went back to the way things were for you before
You and I both know that in your human form,
It will only be more indignity and constant daily ridicule,
Hence why in a blood signature you had sworn revenge against the fools
To gain the power of fifty men, and a charisma greater than that of Zen
So, would you instead prefer to just depart from this earthly plane on a count to ten?"
"Yes," I said, and after the tenth snap of her middle finger, I laid dead

(You told me I was nothing
You all told me I was nothing
No value, No worth,
Nothing special... Re-Birth!
I made a pact with the devil and I sold my soul
And under the full moon light, it's how I roll)

As a titan, As a lycan
As a brokenhearted man-beast
Yeah, it's how I rolled

Mental Rhyme / Mental Song

My ears are closed and my mouth is open
Saliva drips down like a faucet that's been broken
Been busted open with a hammer in a fit of rage
Or like a disease-filled rat that's escaping from an immobile cage
The anger buried deep down explodes more rapidly than the drop of a dime
Everything I ever wished to say to you is now flowing through my mind
And it's releasing into the oblivion in a mental rhyme
Maybe I'll someday tell you, yeah, maybe in good time
But as for right now it will stay locked away in my mind

A Dead Schizophrenic Jew

A perfect human being but perfection is subjective
A dead schizophrenic Jew who was executed for insurrection
It all seems so silly if you attempt any kind of recollection
But at least we have a little book with two millenniums of edit
Said to be the epitome of wisdom even though you've barely even read it
A martyr for the oppressed and a savior for us all
A hero for the meek and an icon for the economic weak
So pass around the basket and donate to 'the cause' (?)
Wallow in wealth in the name of a man without flaws

Better Than Suicide

No more mister nice guy, I'm through playing their games
And being treated like shit, each and every school day
They said I was a nerd, a geek, dweeb and a lame
But now I'm a blood-thirsty monster and I'm ready for fame

A cafeteria full of kids, I surveyed my prey
Their fate now in my hands, oh what a wonderful day
I'm no longer the hunted, the tables have been turned
And I will now release upon them the destruction they have earned

With a pistol to my side, I walked in from the hall
Ready to blast away the first motherfucker that I saw
I took out two jocks and watched them fall to the floor
And then reloaded my gat as she ran for the door
But before she could escape I then smoked his yuppie ass girl

Sitting at one table, I saw a student who wasn't screaming
She just sat there staring with a solemn expression on her face
She had long green hair and pale white skin
A red bra strap and a Black Flag pin

I walked right up to her and put the gun to her head
She just sat there and said "Fuck it, I wouldn't mind being dead"
Frozen in place, I didn't know what to do
"Better than suicide," she added "No one would have a clue"

I looked in her eyes and I saw no fear
Just a tired drained soul and a river of tears
But I couldn't pull the trigger, hell knows why
I told her I was sorry and that I couldn't watch her die

I turned my back and walked back into the hall
Ready to blast away the next student that I saw..

Inferiority Complex

If this was the playground you'd be labeled tattletale or bully
If this was high school you'd be called a pussy
But what are you now? Nothing but a fool
Nothing more, nothing less, bitch
You're just a phony pleaser and goddamn fool
Wearing a plastic badge

Carriage of Death

On this carriage of death, we endlessly ride away from "the left"
On this carriage of death, I wish to see a madam named Riddle Beth
Yet she's smoking crystal meth to the right of me like all of the rest
On this carriage of death carrying the once-considered "best of the best"

On this carriage of death, we know life is only a guess-by-guess test
On this carriage of death, we abandon hope, without a vision to invest
As she's sitting right there in plain sight I am longing to just see her
On this carriage where we all self-abuse until our insides boil, rot and stir

On this carriage of death, it's all really for the best
Nothing ever changes except for the inane details unless
..Unless we turn around and ride back out west

Still onward we ride in fatalism, on this carriage of death

Life On The Run

I wish you could explain
But I know it wouldn't change
It won't ever change a damn thing
Not a single damn thing
It never mattered anyway
And was only worth it for the sting

Is the trash half-empty or is it half-full?
It's probably completely full
And overflowing in an existence so cruel
'Cause I threw it all away, like the barrel of a gun
Or a round of ammunition wasted firing at the rising sun
I left it all behind for a life on the run

Reality was but a dream until I met you
Now I know that nothing is ever as it would seem
The glue holding together my mind, it came apart
Like the shattering of a glass ceramic heart
And all that's left for me is a single-purpose lark
It will take me to a new world away from it all
A place that will leave me breathless and in awe

Still I wonder why
As I stare up at the starry sky
But I guess I'll understand it
On the day I die

Deep Inside

I'm not happy, I try not to smile
I never laugh, but prefer to defile
Demolish your hopes and rationalize your dreams
But deep inside, I pray for insurrection
The destruction of order and a creation so obscene

I'm really not that different, that different from you
You think we have radically dissimilar ways of thinking
Perceptions of self and concepts of wealth

Like a roll of the dice in a game of wits and of stealth
But at the core, it's still always was the same
At the core, not a damn thing has changed

Still a barrier between us forever remains
A barrier I built to filter out undesirables
Which isn't you, so the plan seems to have backfired
But the alienation I release, I guess it stays

Deep in these eyes… Fuck that shit!
Enough of the vague stoney ass metaphor
What is it that lies behind the eyes?
I don't know about you, but I can speak for myself
For me it's filled with darkness, regret and despair
The shadows of all that's been forgotten is what I find there
But what is it that lies behind that?
I can't say I know, not a shit of a clue

I'm really not that different at all from you
You think we are worlds apart, but I don't believe this is true
With incompatible ideas of self
And endlessly clashing conceptions of wealth
Maybe it's because I never tell you that way down deep
I demand the impossible, a brand-new world of chaos and obscenity

A 'soul' may be left over after we die, but it still seems to me
That there's something else inside all of us when we are alive
Is it our thoughts? Our brain? Neuro-fucking-ology?
I won't say I 'believe' it, nor for this one will I argue
But what is it that lies behind what's behind the eyes?

Shakespearean Joker

Just trust me
Try to understand
The path I am taking you
The sensuality of your touch
Let it take me, take you, make us
Thus the sand slipping through my fingers
Lingering seconds calculated by the hourglass
The sundial reads that the day has past
The gravel path we have followed
It all seems so bitter and so hard to swallow

But in a minute, I know,
It is cracked and empty and hollow
I miss you so much, Alone in my head
A midnight swoon but it's all over so soon
Lost in the shadows under the light of the moon
I slit my throat, No thirst for redemption
Merely a taste of the blood I lick off these lips
The innards of the slaughtered goats...

Here, Down Out

I don't wanna leave this room
Or wanna leave this bed
Don't wanna drop to the floor
Just wanna lie here dead
Because if I ever get up
I know it's never enough
So I'll just stay here
Where everything's clear
Don't wanna go over there
Into the lair of terror
I just wanna lay here
In my bed
And in my head
Just in this bed
Down out and dead
With eyes blood red...

At A Party In Hell

I grab a red pen and stick it in my left eye
At a party in hell as our bodies burn and fry
The red ink splatters and camouflages with the blood
I let it drip into my shot of Jack spiked with the seeds from a sack of bud
After I gulp it down I wonder of the life I lived on earth
I think of the living hell I put you through, for what it's worth
Responsibility was a bitch and existence was but a trick
Just a dirty game I gambled away for self-indulgence, QP's and Bic's
Sacrificing all of my dignity and extinguishing any flicker of shame
And apathetic to any misery of yours that was a byproduct of my derange
As I stare into the surrounding flames I know I am dead and out of your hair
It's probably better off this way, without me ever there

But suffering builds character so I guess I made you strong
As I fire up a second bong in hell, my thoughts fall into an aching long
Not a twenty-four hour night goes by that I don't reminisce those days
Yet does my departure give you any grief or are you ecstatic with the change?
I guess that when it's all said and done, nothing began, and no one won
And when your legacy falls to the ground, there's not a damn place to run
And when everything hits the fan, life was no more than just a fantasy land
With nothing real to understand or cherish but only an emptiness to feel
You can thank the eternal cycle that your joy is no longer mine to steal
As I take my last shot of Jack and then put down the bong
At a party in hell where I'm lost in a never-ending mental song

("I was never much for earthly parties either...")

Roadside Story

She didn't seem unobtainable and yet was gorgeous nevertheless
The way she smiled and she laughed made her seem nothing like the rest
But as it later turned out, she fed me bullshit and sugar-coated lies
And then strung me along like a glued together string of wingless flies

Oh, I didn't mean to kill her, you must believe me when I say this
But when I saw her face again, something overtook me and I had to fucking taste it
With my peddle to the floor she tried to run but didn't get very far
Her body flew forward and to the ground upon the impact of my speeding car

I kneeled down and held her in my arms as she slowly bled to death
It was clear she didn't even have a dozen heartbeats left
I let the tears fall like the blood and then looked up at the darkened sky
Screaming random vulgarities out to no one as the voices just wondered why

As the police lights are now flashing from behind, I can hear the sirens blasting
And feel the anger building up inside me as I see the gawkers slowly passing
I don't know what to do, no, I haven't got a clue
They're coming at me with their handcuffs and their clubs and tasers too

Well, I ain't going back to prison, they ain't taking my ass alive
So I reach into my pocket and pull out my trusty forty-five
Laughing like a hyena I tell the motherfuckers to bring it on
But as the bullets penetrate my skin I guess it didn't last very long

I fall to the ground beside her, beside the woman that I killed
And slowly close my eyes and lay to rest with hardly a single dream fulfilled

As my existence fades to black I cry out what I still have left to say
"Fuck you all!" I conclusively scream to a cruel world in decay

<u>All Saints Day</u>

There once was a man named Henry Dankenstein
He was a peculiar fellow searching for the light and seventh sign
Yet from the outside world he always liked to stay confined
He sat in the basement all night in front of his typewriter
Sipping his coffee, and sometimes a glass of apple cider
He was a smart lad with a touch of sad
He was a kind lad with a bit of bad
Dankenstein, he was a man of his word
Locked away for ten syllables, it was so absurd
Censored for his creation and his own personal salvation
His thirst for answers had lead him to supposed damnation
And in prison he acquired the alias of:
Nosferatu A ROF Inspiration

I relate to monsters because I am one, yeah
I relate to demons because they're in us all
As I'm blazing down the road on Halloween night
I see them on the sidewalk, feeling alright

There once was a manifesto, it had no title, just the author's name
It was written by Dankenstein, no really, he was very much insane
Some titled it "Frankenstein" and this always annoyed a playa named Stacula
Stacula always dressed in black, yet mild-mannered as a matter of fact
He pretended to respect society's customs, hiding his inner bat
He lived alone in a mansion on the top of a hill
Rumored across the land to be a bloodsucker who just may kill
The stories were all believed despite being fantastic, it's true
All were welcome in his abode, this was quite clear, everyone knew
Outcasted by the world and hardened into nothing
But it all became okay when he drank and drank, oh it was something
It couldn't be avoided for it was his very essence of survival
To carry on, it was much needed, it was vital
Such a lonely existence, this one of Stacula
But he never drank... Wine

I relate to monsters because I am one, yeah
I relate to demons because they're in us all
As I'm blazing down the road on Halloween night

I see them on the sidewalk, feeling alright

There once was a dead motherfucker named Nosferatu
A rebirth had transformed him into a creature of the night
Rejecting religious claims as to the amorality of temptation
Misunderstood and said to be evil, eyes in dilation
Women were known to swoon merely from his gaze
(He also dug the kush, blueberry and purple haze)
Lurking each night through the Underground streets
Physically he was nothing but mentally not to be beat
And every now and then a madam fell into his heat
Deep in his eyes would emerge a burning into her soul
And after drinking them dry, it was time for another bowl
Longing the life he once had, instead of it being all the same
Nosferatu was his name, his very name, it chills the veins

I relate to monsters because I am one, yeah
I relate to demons because they're in us all
As I'm blazing down the road on Halloween night
I see them on the sidewalk, feeling alright

Officer Santa

You better not shout, You better not pout
Your better hope you don't die, I'm telling you why
Officer is click-clicking your life

He's making a disk, He's checking it twice
He's gonna grope you if you're naughty or nice
Officer is frisking your town

You Better Watch Out

He makes his living by cheap elf labor
He doesn't have to pay his taxes
Life is great for him where he works
But tonight in your town he lurks

Oh, you better watch out
I said, you better watch out
'Cause Santa Claus is coming
To town

He watches through your window
He knows you palmed that dough
He knows how he can blackmail you
So you must fear him don't you know

Oh, you better watch out
I said, you better watch out
'Cause Santa Claus is coming
Tonight

He sees you when you're sleeping
He has his hand down there and rubbing
He knows all of your preferences
But he only cares for kiddy peeping

Oh, you better watch out
And you better not doubt
'Cause Santa Claus is coming
To town

Nomad

He awakens on a boulder shadowed by a covered bridge above him
And to the sunlight shining down onto the glistening creek in front of him
He stands tall and stretches and greets the new day
And trods down to the streaming water but it all just tastes so sour
Without a place to call home in a world where he roams

No shoes or socks on his feet, he steps into the shallow creek
Feeling the pebbles between his toes and the tickle of splashing water
He had awoken from another nightmare of a torturous past
He hasn't eaten in two days and wonders if today could be his last
With the laws of the jungle and involuntary fasts

He once had it all, a wife and two kids and a college degree
But after a fatal car crash he was never the same
He was left all alone and abandoned, just screaming in copeless agony
He got fired from his job and lost his money and his home
But now he's a wandering nomad in a world where he roams

As the sun is setting in the sky up above an endless highway
He stands on the side of the road and is hoping to hitch a ride
The hours soon pass and not a single car appears

But his faith that he'll survive has yet to be phased
He straps back on his knapsack and trods back the way he came

It was a childhood fantasy but even as a grown man he would daydream
Sometimes on the drive home from work his mind would drift to the surreal
He wondered what life would be like to live off of the land
And never have to worry about the bills, his debts or student loans
But now it's a reality in this world where he roams

Dr. Seuss Was Gangsta

Curiosity killed the cat
But cats have nine lives so it's kinda wack
The cat came back and bought a hat
She went to town and met a bat

"What is it that killed you, Mrs. Cat?"
"My thirst for answers, Dr. Bat"
"Well, I have very unique evolutionary ties
Some say I'm the perfect example of creationist lies"
"Cool, nice to meet you, now I know it's a guise"

The bat flew away and went to the cave
But on his way, he past the rave
The human raver looked up at the bat
On LSD, it was hella phat
"Was that an angel, the mothman or a bat?"
"I don't know, let's break out the crack"

The other raver broke out the crack
Middle name Dubya, a first and last one he lacked
"I like this crack, it's where it's at"
"I like it too, but I don't like this annoying gnat"

The gnat was buzzing around his head
He swatted it dead before he could hear what it said
And then he also dropped a dog in its head
He knew in spite of any dissent he must attack Baghdad
Yeah, it was several years later, but still pretty bad

Sex, Drugs, Power and Murder

[Introduction:]
Do you mind if I tell you all a story?
You can always leave the room if you find it too gory.
It's about three individuals and the tangled web that they weaved.
Three individuals, a nihilist philosopher, a dark eyed freak, and a teenage siren.
It just may shock, terrify, and choke you up until you can barely breath.
Hence why I am preemptively warning you,
And you're always completely free to leave...

[One Rebel Of Forever:]
Sitting in my basement, in the dark alone
I was watching the idiot box
Until I was startled by the telephone
It snapped me out of focus, it pulled me from my zone
I decided to ignore it 'cause at 3.A.M it wouldn't be known
But a half an hour later, it started to ring again
This time around I rose, I rose up from my bed
After picking it up, I began to listen to every word intently
The tone and rhythm, it was shaky yet hypnotic
But hearing the meaning, I responded anything but gently
She said that by this time tomorrow I may or may not be dead
With a jeweled dagger to my chest or a .44 caliber in my head
She didn't specify, or even say hello, but I still knew just who it was
A high school sweetheart of mine from way back when
She always knew perfectly how to adapt to her surroundings and blend
The last time I had seen her neither of us even gave a wave
But now she was on fragmented rant I wasn't entirely sure just how to make
"Come to my funeral, come with me to my grave"
"I can no longer take the infliction I endlessly crave"
Clearly insane, but then again, a mania like this, it's somewhat tame
Back in the day, I remember worse, it's just the functionality of her brain
Like having me smear her whole body, until covered in sloshed wolfsbane
Two days later, authorities found me hanging from my bedroom fan
Switch the blade and cut the rope, and on someone else I land
I was off to pick up an eighth of herb, but had gotten a little tied up
And seven feet below was a bed, throat, wrist and blood-coated cup

It' all about Sex,
Drugs, Power, and Murder
Just Sex,
Drugs, Power, and Murder
I said, Drugs, Drugs,

Sex, Power, and Murder

I lust Sex, Drugs, Power, and Murder

[Nosferatu:]
The squawk of the raven echoes as the clock strikes midnight
And I'm kneeling in the dirt under the illuminating full moon light
In front of me is a gravestone and I am slowly brushing off the dust
I'm Nosferatu, bitch, don't snitch, but Drugs Murder and Sex I lust
But right now, partake in any of the above is nowhere on my mind
Just an old dead homie of mine who departed back in seventeen-oh-nine
Forgotten by all except for me, but I guess that's just how it is, over time
We all have to die someday, except for those cursed to forever walk the earth
Shit, dawg, shoot me in the fucking eye and I'll survive, for what it's worth
Turn around as this peculiar 'watchman' approaches, I was trespassing in these parts
The cemetery is apparently closed every night when it gets to be this dark
The proceeding surprise in her eyes and the blood from her veins ingested like a lark
It was enough, for at least the time being, to soothe my blackened heart

It's all about Sex,
Drugs, Power, and Murder
Just Sex,
Drugs, Power, and Murder
I said, Drugs, Drugs,
Sex, Power, and Murder

I want Sex, Drugs, Power, and Murder.

[The Stone Angel (ie: 'Cindy Folaski'):]
I was writing a poem in the back of my art class
Just smoked a joint in the bathroom and was high off my ass
Not paying any attention to the monotone of this idiot
Douche-bag hick! And he knows it! Just fuck this shit!
After the bell rang, he decided to pull me aside
A few words in private about my failing grade, he lied
He grabbed me by the waist and pushed me against the wall
Blood tricked down my back but that most certainly wasn't all
After my head slammed hard, he put one hand under my blouse
And before I could scream, he put his other one over my mouth
He said a racial slur, it was two words, it had a 'w' and an 'er'
Two or so minutes later I heard a page which he ignored
But still in the pause, I pulled from my pocket all I adored
A razor I had on my left wrist just seven hours beforehand
Would a kid like me even be believed, yeah, would he be canned?
This crossed my mind for an instant, but it had no leg on which to stand

With the blade now to his throat, he laughed as if it was a joke
But with a quick swipe, I then smoked the fucker like a toke

It's all about Sex,
Drugs, Power, and Murder
Just Sex,
Drugs, Power, and Murder
I said, Drugs, Drugs,
Sex, Power, and Murder

I crave Sex, Drugs, Power, and Murder.

[Outroduction:]
You can't say I didn't warn you.
But it was all in good fun, all in good fright.
Pleasant dreams, my wide-eyed friends.
Just don't let the bed bugs get you in the night...

On the Down Low

What do you mean?
Do I look high?
In this apartment
In this kitchen
Look in my eyes
Do you think I'm high?
You have no idea

Wake n' Bake
Piss and shake
Stay blazed all day
And every day
Slang herb yourself
For dough to pay

What do you mean?
I smoked three bowls
Before I went
To the train station
To meet up with you
You have no idea
How much
You have no clue

Wake n' Bake
Piss and shake
Stay blazed all day
Every day

Are you hearing this?
Yeah, you were talking
About high and sober
And sober and high
Yada, yada, yada..

Habits

How is it five o' clock?
In the afternoon?
This makes me want to sleep even more

I get out of my bed
Where the fuck's my glasses?
I'm fucking blind!
Where the hell's my glasses?

Check my MySpace, There's nothing new
And remember I left my Newports
In the car last night

It's pouring rain, I'm on the porch
A swig of Monster, I light my smoke
And start the day
Feeling good? Not so much

Know Smoking

Light it up, your first cig
Take the drag, it stimulates
Inhale quick, You feel big

Indulgence and lungs that rot
It's so sexy, it's so hot
Stinky breath and smokers cough
It's so sexy, it is not

Cigarette, oh Cigarette
How I love to fucking hate you
Newport short, oh Newport short
How you never leave or even criticize

Yellow teeth and smokers cough
It keeps me going, but maybe not?
Smelly clothes and lungs that rot
It's what I want, but can I stop?

Cigarette, oh Cigarette
How I never will betray you
Nicotine, oh Nicotine
I take you in and let you control

Cataclysmic

Force-fed falsehoods drip slowly down my lips
Like the first taste of blood ingested with a demonic kiss
As I stare fiercely into the moon I am lost in its comfort and bliss
Like a broken bleeding heart or the sipping of a slit wrist
The last one standing in this conflict will be a martyr or a plague
Sweeping across the land, their message subjective and vague
Yet we all take it in and expect our own selfish interests to be granted
And the ulterior motives, corruption and greed forever remain slanted

Burn burn burn it down
Fall fall fall to the ground
The end is near, a screeching sound
Chaos surrounds, the balance impounds
As it burns burns to the ground

The anti-Christ of rationality sought, but when they are caught
Thus the trial and removal of those on the hierarchal top
Exposed for their lies one may hope to someday stop
An uproar for the oppressed to reclaim their deserved and desired lot
This obtuse reality some see approaching is only a matter of time
A revolutionary dream forgotten and buried in the ashes of mental rhyme
It washes over me like the winter breeze or like an agonizing derange
Or like a bullet through my chest and its resulting fortune and fame

Burn burn burn it down
Fall fall fall to the ground

The end is near, a screeching sound
Chaos surrounds, the balance impounds
As it burns burns to the ground

A rising new world for which I walk the paradoxical line
Good and evil declared as fabricated concepts rejected in my mind
But I still can drop to my knees crying out for a halt to all of the misery
Like an exploding meteor demolishing a landmark of dire history
Or a shooting star adding a sense of beauty in the moonlit sky
Or an insane agony leaving nihilistic confusion and the question of "why?"
Redistribution of power and an end to all of the madness
But what will it take to push past my own cataclysmic sadness?

Snitches

I see the suburbs
and the homogeneity of it all
I see the conveniently located tree
The sparrow and his lady bird
It's the middle of the night
and they like to tell me that the cops don't bite
But most of all... I see snitches

I see the flashing lights
And I see the seven joints
They were rolled with the papers
complementarily sold in a pouch of Kite
I see the road block
I see an illegal search
But most of all... I see snitches

I see the attention seeker
I see the grim reaper
I look in the mirror into the reflecting mirror
and I see Nosferatu
dissuading the perception as a keeper
I see the bared fangs, the mic and the axe
But most of all... I see snitches

I see the city boy
with a spray can and half-O sack
As I pass him on the sidewalk
I see the rummage through his back pack

I see the gun and badge
I see the custom glass
But most of all... I see snitches

I nod my head and tell you
I see a lot of things
That I do
I see the innocence I once possessed
and the remaining bit of it left
I see the departed soul
But most of all... I see snitches

Schwag

In a public place,
The transaction was quick
You left the scene,
Before I knew I'd been gypped
One glance at the sack,
And it was pretty damn wack
...You sold me schwag!
...You sold me schwag!

Thirty five for a "quarter"
Twenty bucks for an "eighth"
Two eighths make a quarter
Half a quarter, an eighth
And yet I now have to smoke,
Twice as much of the 'weight'
(Or half as much of the dank),
For the same degree of affect
I fire it up and reflect
...You sold me schwag!
…You sold me schwag!

I don't mean to rag
But before I even opened the bag
I didn't even give it a whiff
Certainly no hit
I just looked at the shit,
And already knew it
...You sold me schwag!
...You sold me schwag!

Why the fuck did I pay,
That extra fifteen
For approximately the some serving,
Of THC in the green?
And shittier blaze, even if the high's just as mean
...You sold me schwag!
...You sold me schwag!

Born with A Cigarette in Her Mouth

An insignificant bug splattered and smeared on my windshield
Wiping off the guts with a scrape and then a yield
There she was fully visible in my rear view mirror
Her tear-struck eyes and fist bared up at the sky
Cussing out a cold world she quite clearly despised
I continue cruising on, trying to ignore it and turned up the volume to the song
Was it an Anti-Flag song preaching how to make the world get more along?
In a society full of pain and the now falling rain
Dripping from the sky and concealing her tearful cry
Only left remaining is the sight of a fist bared in passionate anger
But our last words weren't exactly: "Don't be a stranger"
I hope she doesn't see that I'm about twenty yards in front of her
I wonder if she still believes all evil is found in meat and fur
And even if she did, would she even recognize "that kid"
Puffing on a Port and listening to Twiztid?

'Cause she was born with a cigarette in her mouth
A Marlboro Red cigarette in her mouth
Drag after drag, Smoke exhaled out the snout
Lick after lick and stroke after stroke
Light up another smoke and know what it's all about
She was born with a cigarette in her mouth

I wanted to kiss her so bad every second I was with her
I wanted to love her and hold her as together we riled up a stir
Two rebels with a cause rejecting any social codes or laws
In a society of unnecessary repugnance and never-ending list of flaws
Youthful ideals in a world so obscene
With her hair florescent green as a counter-culture teen
We were hopping on the train of life to naïve hopes and dreams
Laughing at passerby's following the school into the net
At the anglers and complacent yuppies who you could always bet
Would never stand alone to fight for what they knew was right

Unless it was against a business with shopping hours they spite
Superficial teenage bullshit and we were a part of it
But it still felt like a light shining from above releasing a certain dove
A strong sense of warmth whenever in her presence
And would have given anything for just three seconds of evanescence
But I knew I wasn't good enough for her to let me be any more
And after she had gone, my whole body went numb yet sore
But now today as I turn the corner, she again drops out of sight
But just as I do, she pulls out a black Bic light

'Cause she was born with a cigarette in her mouth
A Marlboro Red cigarette in her mouth
Drag after drag, Smoke exhaled out the snout
Lick after lick and stroke after stroke
Light up another smoke and know what it's all about
She was born with a cigarette in her mouth

Rise of The Underdog

A galaxy in my eyes
Swirling and colliding deep inside
My soul pains, Destructive urge in my heart
Longing for the molding to never end or start
The world I know of inspiration
Will not help me in this mind state of creation
But I know what I must do
Embrace a forgotten reality of external obtuse
I walk into the light of social madness and chaos
And fall out of the paining cycle of darkness
As I embrace this light I can feel the scalding acid rain
Dropping from the sky and becoming one with my derange
The struggle begins
The world can feel it

Drop a Dime

The darkness is inside me
Boiling like the iron
Blinding light surrounds me
Burning my eyes and molding a figurine
The disconnect collides, I drop a dime
Into the toll deep in these eyes

A purchase for two more 'pack of lies'
War toys played with by frat boys
But it's all a guise
And all of the reasons were nothing but
A 'pack of lies'

As the vampires stare into this light
Darkness personified and rejected outside
Facing the incoming and outward collide
An explosion of the soul

I drop a dime in the death toll deep inside
A forsaken and eternal aftermath
Of the great demise
Surviving dead buried in my head
Yet still alive
As I drop a dime

The darkness is inside me
The blinding light surrounds me
I squint my eyes as the disconnect collides
And deep in these eyes
I drop a dime

Dagger
(With a photograph by Nick Ulanowski)

A dagger by the window
A dagger through the soul
No rainbow or heaven just a dagger so cold

A dagger in my eye
A dagger of disguise
Fear and rejection of the world outside

A dagger through my heart
A dagger for a bowl
It's breaking up the bud and slicing up the mold

A dagger blocking sunlight
A dagger for a scrape and roll
For if I open this window I'd be letting go the cold

A dagger invades my eye
It's a dagger of a lie
Surviving in this dark room but will I live 'till twenty-five?

A dagger on my wrist
A dagger in my other fist
Drawing blood without a trace but either way without a miss

A dagger used to pick a rose
A dagger unleashed on all my foes
This world outside is now embraced despite the window being closed

Boyz in The Burbs
(a parody of Eazy E's "Boyz in The Hood")

Wake up at noon, bright and ready to start the day
It's another re-run, I pop in the tape and then hit "play"
I gotta get stoned
Before the day begins

And before my parents starts bitching
About the rent
I put the bong down and then take my piss
Brew some coffee and slit my wrist
While the blood's dripping I get an epiphany
I go off to the shop and pick up a TEVO for me
In the back of the school, I open the sack
But I gotta have the right pipe to smoke this crack
Well I guess that for now I'm still on re-play
So it's back to the crib and I start the day

'Cause the boyz in the burbs are always hard
Taking out the trash to a curb so far
Know nothing in life but to be legit
Don't quote me, boy, I ain't no snitch

Bored as hell and I wanna get ill
So I go to a place where some homies chill
Fellas out there trying to make that dollar
Roll up a gram in two Phillies per hour
Greeted with a Faygo and I start drinking
A caffeine pill and damn, I'm tweakin'
Clock out at six and wake up with a body shake
Dazed and wondering if to my date I'm too late
Back to the house and then kick back
Light a Newport and itch my crack
Look at my cell and find out I missed it
So gotta get to her house for a Merry Christmas
But first to FTD for my special present
I know she'll find this bouquet quite pleasant
But on the way over I didn't click it
So those damn pigs gave me a ticket

'Cause the boyz in the burbs are always hard
Taking out the trash to a curb so far
Know nothing in life but to be legit
Don't quote me, boy, I ain't said shit

'Cause the boyz in the burbs are always hard
Taking out the trash to a curb so far
Know nothing in life but to be legit
Don't quote me, boy, I ain't said shit

Bored as hell and I wanna get ill
So please drop this blog a comment as I pack this kill

With my trusty corn cob, I don't fuck with the glass one
Just a few rips left and gotta go on another bud run

'Cause the boyz in the burbs are always hard
Taking out the trash to a curb so far
Know nothing in life but to be legit
Don't quote me, boy, I ain't no snitch

Two Broken Toyz and A Girl Named Gail
(or: "Boys in The Burbs pt. 2")

[A Toy of the Light:]
Wake up bright and early to the shining sunlight
It's the time of the night I feel most alright
I think to myself about my
Martyred existence
And how I refuse to go out
Without a little resistance
I stagger to the phone to call this girl named Gail
She's the one with 'good times' for sale
I proceed to dial that triple-five
Then a "six"-"six"-"six" and the "one" still alive
I guess she's not there as it goes to voicemail
I was supposed to use my last slug in a 'would-be sale'
She's clearly not there, but what about my gun
with a Jesus sticker and a smiley-face sun?
Well Great One, it looks like I have failed
So I pull the trigger and my body goes frail

'Cause the toyz of the light, They ain't uptight
They just have their own callings and battles to fight
Like killing a bitch selling chains and whips
What else they got if they can't burn a witch?

[A Toy of The Dark:]
Clock out bright and early to the shining sunlight
Wake up to the robins by the window greeting the night
I think to myself in regards to
These wrongs to right
And how I refuse to just die
Without a damn good fight
I stumble to the phone and pick it up
But before I do I gotta have a quick puff

I put out my joint and dial that triple-five
Then a "four"-"two"-"zero" and the "one" I strive
I reach the recording: "Hi. You've reached Gail"
I redial to discover she was shanked in jail
Another one I love gone, it's nothing new
I wipe my tears and crack a morning brew
And then over my head it shatters in two
But it's such a bore and I'm digging some more
So I grab the phone and extend the cord
Wrap around my neck and finish the chore

'Cause the toyz of the dark, They ain't got a heart
Just a box of spliffs and notepad of larks
Like a hit list they smear with shit
Then hang themselves with this 'how to' kit

I feel so sick as everything now spins
And wonder if in life one ever wins
I extend my wings and take to the sky
Whisper "goodbye" and then ask "why?"

'Cause the toyz of the light, They ain't uptight
They just have their own callings and own battles to fight
Some wronging their wrongs, Some stealing our rights
Some turn to the rear and drop out of sight

(and) The toyz of the dark, They ain't got a heart
Just a box of spliffs and notepad of larks
Some fighting for rights, Some living in spite
Some turn to the rear and drop out of sight

Gateway

If eyes are the gateway to the soul
Then how come this portal lacks shine or gold?
If I revise a universe to escape this cold
Will it end with darkness or light as our lives unfold?

If darkness within darkness is the gateway
I shall open this door and enter the pathway
If darkness within darkness is the gateway
The gateway to all understanding
Of ourselves and rejections?

Of our lives and reflections?
A banding human race in good shape and standing
When you look in *these eyes*
What do you see? Personal misery?

A rebirth from inside...

I travel up and beyond expanding into the night
Through this twisted tunnel awaiting the definitive light
In a deep state of fright as I'm losing my might
Faces now surround me who are here to hurt me
They want to coerce me and refuse to show mercy

Twists and turns with no end in sight
Toward the outcome claimed as blinding and bright
Images now collide in galaxies of mass
And times that have vanished on a spectrum so vast
A bearded man with a transcript declaring weeks for fast
I see warring armies and lions eating fleshy trash
They were deemed as crass in this distant past
How come this identity never did last?

If darkness within darkness is the gateway
I shall open this door and enter the pathway
If darkness within darkness is the gateway
The gateway to all understanding
And social banding
Of petty existence? Of creative resistance?
As I stare into *the campfire* **upon coming dawn**
What is it I see? A baby bird set free?

Or an endless good time...

Looking into the flames I dig deeper for meaning
Until all that is left is but a pure conscious of being
I see the galaxies afar and an isolated star
A star made of plastic seen by all as fantastic
And a gripped bone that is never deemed drastic
The faces surround me but none there to bluff me
As some dare to love me while these others swear to cuff me

Listening more intently to the crackle of flame
Now embracing what is a cackle of insane
And a beating rhythm by a setting of stone drums
And a scalding rain of acid bleeding our gums

The fire continues to extinguish, and it is turning tiresome
The sharp tones of the drums beat on and on
Rising out of one it now begins to come
Extending higher and higher is the venomous snake
A hiss and rattle is released against all those faces who forsake
Thus a conclusive battle yet eternal ache

If eyes are the gateway to the soul
Then how come this portal lacks shine or gold?
For a revision of a new world to know
I enter the pathway and see death unfold

Put It Down
(With a photograph by Nick Ulanowski)

My name doesn't matter
In a world so scattered
I jerk my head around and then push forth
A lack of love and flow of warmth
A society of complacency to others pain
Exclusion and alienation
Injustice and abomination
But my name is Nick
I dress in black
And I'm just the idealist they say must be on crack
But there are others who fight
And there are those with might

I raise a glass to the anti-hero
We all need that nonsensical soul
I raise a glass to the cynical philosopher
To those in power, You're way too smart
I raise a glass to the activist...
Because I'm putting it down for those with heart

I look around and see the pain
Everyone just breathing another day
This isn't how we have to live
An individual has so much more to give
To give to society other than money
Prestige is worthless in reality, honey
Let's rise above from the ashes
Stand together and love each other

I raise a glass to the anti-hero
We all need that nonsensical soul
I raise a glass to the cynical philosopher
To those in power, You're way too smart
I raise a glass to the activist...
Because I'm putting it down for those with heart

I watch smog rise from a blackness of burned-out hope
Through the clouds, Into the night without cope
No care at all, Just to spite
Middle finger high and ignoring the cry
Giving up without a fight
But that's no way to live the life
Stand up for what's right and conquer the strife
Use your compassion but don't forget smart

I put it down for those with heart

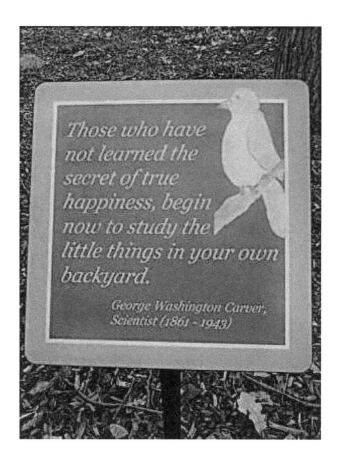

Introspection

I embrace in my soul a quest for introspection
And deep in my eyes is a burning reflection

The reality of existence is a farce
The existence of reality is subjective
...And fading into a life of never-ending dream

Darkness and derange, I see the sorrow, regret and pain
Am I socially insane or just in deserving of universal blame
For all I have done and all I have become
Cursing and denying the rising sun
Or is it that life has only begun?

The existence of reality is subjective
The reality of existence is a farce
...And transforming into a mindset of chaos and nothingness

Deep in my eyes I stare into a burning reflection
And I embrace in my soul a quest for introspection

Room Number Zero

Hotel hermit hears a lot
In room number zero steers a plot
Utopian fear and love sought
Dodging cops and smoking pot

On a scent-easy spot
Surrounding cops and robots
Three hits of this pot
His worst time to get caught

Mental song non-stop
Room number zero, Dare not
As robot clerk was shot
Dodging cops and toking lots

Aimless run non-stop
Snitch on deck sees the pot
Sobbing girl and a cop
Her worst time to get caught

A productive blood clot
Or just a moving blue dot
In room number zero
Dodging cops and smoking pot

Hazy Fire

Sitting around a campfire
Holding a wonderful girl
Transcendence of emotional warmness
Physical manifestation of affection
Blood running slowly
Lost in a daze

Psychoactive downer
Herbal fucking painkiller
Mary Jane, Ganja Bud
Pack it in and blaze
Feel the open haze

Functional Scatterbrains

They're functional scatterbrains, Functional scatterbrains
Two faces without a name, They're functional scatterbrains
Going into total plain with chunky matter on insane
Going into denial of pseudo-sane with laughter on the brain
Cause the mind's gotta have a say if you want to see today
So put the flame out with a cane and fire up a "nay"
"Say, or" is it an existence of random and delay?
Functional Scatterbrains, Functional Scatterbrains
They're functional scatterbrains living each they're own repay
Whether claims of harmony or derange still pockets full of pain
Kitchen pipes full of drain and dirt sacks full of rain
Like a girl on the mind of lost confine
Or forgotten define into scattered bits of rhyme
Whether sober all day and high all night
Or high all awake and sober alright
They're aware of the pain and just differ in beats of insane
They're either puffing on the pain or breathing on another day
They're functional scatterbrains, functional scatterbrains

Breath In, Tweak Out

Fire that shit up
Stall on the pass and take a puff
It's all good
No need for hope
It's alright
Cope up in smoke
It goes up in smoke
Light up a square after the toke

I was stoned to death last night

The ghastly image flashes
Forgotten dreams, ripped flesh and gashes
As my whole life passes before my eyes
It passes me by on the detour,
Is there nothing more?
Is there nothing more
than the eternity that's been endured?
It's up in smoke, I can't explain
Only the ashes of all that remain
Nothing inside
Except for demise

I was stoned to death last night

That's right, I was stoned to death last night
Everyone died, deep in my eyes
I was stoned to death last night

Bears, Bees, Trees and Me

The bear in my garage is clawing my hair
He came from his lair just to scare
But I'm not afraid of that stupid bear!
I grabbed an acetylene torch and cooked him rare
I then went to his lair and tagged all the walls
Burned all the leaves and set up some stalls
After ending his terror I pissed right in there
And went outside and pissed everywhere
Marking my territory oh, what a wondrous sight!
But then something happened again that just wasn't right

A bee hoard flew down coming after me
But it's my territory now, You stupid bees!
But they began to sting me instead of Stan Lee!
So I threw an M-80 and blew up the tree
With their hive gone the bees decided to flee
But with territory missing I fell to my knees
Crying out, "Why, oh why, you maniac bees!"
I used all my strength and began to rise
Wiped my tears and put my fist in the sky
Oh, who cares, it's just a dumb forest
I then met up with a nymph and partied with Chuck Norris!
Thus the moral of this story so gory
Always bring your torch if it ain't a quarry

A Sappy 'Love' Poem

Her eyes are green like a windy meadow
Her skin is yellowish like a name in the snow
Her pupils are black like Rodney King
Her voice sounds like an all-time favorite song
And her hair smells wonderful like an eighth of kush

Her soul is pure like 100% bleach
Her spirit is strong like the Incredible Hulk
Her heart pumps blood like a breathing machine
Her mind is beautiful like a garden of black roses
And her name rings in my head like the *goddamn* telephone

Thoughts of Lenore

If I ever want to feel bad about myself I will drop you a line
If I ever want to be called a nasty name I'll know exactly who's inclined
I'll know exactly where to turn, I'll know exactly what to do
But as for right now I just wish I could halt these endless thoughts of you

Lying on my bed with these angry thoughts of Lenore
I shall now quote the Raven, "Nevermore.."

Porcelain dolls gripped in my palms and heroin needles in my veins
She possesses such a tender skin like a swarm of maggots eating brains
I give the heads a twist and I close both of my eyes
And then drift off to sleep only to dream of her demise

Mind screaming in agony with these thoughts of Lenore
I'd hate to quoth the Raven but "Nevermore.."

Not ever again, no, never again
Not ever again, "Nevermore.."

Poets Are Assholes

("Two lines, Two lines...") ("It was an eight-stanza poem though")
("Hold up, where'd I leave that fucking pen?")

I like being narcissistic, I am my favorite self-critic
I think I'm masochistic and love it for her to go ballistic
I hate the stinkin' cops, I think it's okay for the bacon to rot
Actually, I'm vegetarian but I waste food an awful lot
I like being selfish and I like eating shellfish
I like to wear badass leather
And tell you that my Sierra Club sticker is so much better
I like being confusing, I hate being misunderstood
I once hit a guy in the face with a log in the deep dark woods
I like inside jokes, I light my cigarette after the toke
But if you mention that incident one more time
When you're not looking
I'll defecate in your van and on the seat put out my smoke

("Shit dawg, ya got the record?") ("Damn straight")
("Skanking, shanking and danking... Juggalo, Juggalo")

POETS ARE ASSHOLES, Yeah, I said it
POETS ARE ASSHOLES, Don't mind you re-read it
POETS ARE ASSHOLES, Word up! I get it
POETS ARE ASSHOLES, And don't you forget it!
POETS ARE ASSHOLES, I'm sorry, can you repeat that?
WRITERS ARE ASSHOLES

(*flicks lighter*) (*crumples up notebook paper*)

I like being iconoclastic, I like ideas to be drastic
And I can't help but notice this voluntary servitude is quite fantastic
I like Dennis Leary, I like those commercials that ask if now you can hear me
And every time I see the ending to "King Kong" I get a little teary
I like to roll up green shiny stuff, I love the orange Zig-Zag's
I smoke it to the butt and then it's either a cig or I burn a flag

I don't ever burn that one to the crisp, because, really, that's bad!
You have to understand that I'm sometimes short on rags
I like to smoke cigarettes, They taste a lot like licorice
I like to 'force rhyme' and cuss and have an excuse to say "clitoris"
I like free range, organic chicken and I like wearing mittens
I like to stain them with the poultry blood and claim it's Paris Hilton's
I hate people who wear fur, I hate people who dress up their dogs
I think drunk drivers have the IQ of a bur or evergreen logs
I like to dissent you and I like to offend you
I like to make you scratch your head and wonder
Whether or not I just ascended you

("Dear Dayna Garcia, How I miss you so...")
("Damn. I was found out!") ("You're supposed to ward off the evil spirits!")

POETS ARE ASSHOLES, Yeah, I said it
POETS ARE ASSHOLES, Don't mind you re-read it
POETS ARE ASSHOLES, Word up! I get it
POETS ARE ASSHOLES, And don't you forget it!
POETS ARE ASSHOLES, I'm sorry, can you repeat that?
ARTISTS ARE ASSHOLES

("The dagger of pain and destruction") ("The rose of delicacy and creation")
("My eyes are burning but I still can't find my pen...")

Fox News

Single mother is not on the show
R. Murdoch owns the station you know
So you watch held-down defend the social moat
He's just traitorous vile, Welfare's real style
Social moat and black man
A talking-head turncoat
Host of the show assents, how low
So we listen to the turncoat
Rupert Murdoch owns this "throw"
The billionaire without a soul
In his pockets, Corporate vile
It's to suppress the social rile
His power says 'preserve the dough'
Single mother is not on the show

Starved for Attention

Starved for attention when you've hit rock bottom
Starved for attention so what's the fucking problem?
Starved for attention and falling faster every day
Starved for attention and searching for a way
Starved for attention with a gun in your hand
Starved for attention with blood in the sand
Starved for attention as a teenager of Sodom
Starved for attention when you've hit rock bottom
Starved for attention so who's the fucking problem?

(Not us of course)

Never Enough

She's at her apartment with the demons they invoked
And is loading up a glock 'cause she's ready to smoke
Fingering the trigger with the barrel to her head
Ready to end it all with suicide, she's seeing red

It's not that it wasn't good enough, it's not that at all
But it still wasn't perfect enough for a single one of y'all

He fires up a joint, sitting out on his porch
Residing on the end of an empty road
The stars shine bright as does the moon
As he's surrounded by trees, wolves, crickets and raccoons

It's not that it wasn't good enough, it's not that at all
It just wasn't perfect enough for anyone of y'all

Trapped in my own mind, I wanna get away
I don't wanna leave this bed and face it all today
I want these thoughts to disappear like a leaf carried in the wind
Yet still I remain immobile like a rock, wondering "when will it end?"

It's not that it wasn't good enough, it's not that at all
But it still wasn't perfect enough for a single one of ya'll

Yeah, it still wasn't perfect enough so fuck all y'all

Interwoven

The bullet flies freely through the night
Unnoticeable to the naked eye, only to spite
Into the chest of the newly departed, after fall of night
It has come, for a new phase of the cycle has begun
No longer to wander the streets, but released from the gun
Was it an amorality? Or merely an equilibrium in tune?
If only time will tell, under the light of the moon

Death begins at life, for some
Life begins at death, for many
...Or so we believe, or so they perceive

Love ends at death, for some
Death ends at love, for many
...Or so they believe, or so we perceive

"What is it?" he asks, about this evil that still lurks
The room stays silent and refuses to give him the works
Until one single voice tells him the reality not to be reprimanded
"The Count's existence has ended, but his infliction will never be mended"
The shadow of his castle continues to haunt them, fear-stricken of the unknown
"Darkness falling across the countryside," it is exclaimed in a forceful tone
The traveler is told it is not his concern so be gone
"Just leave us in peace, pay for your drink and move on"

Life ends at life, for many
Death begins at death, for some
...Or so they believe, or so we perceive

Death ends at death, for many
Love begins at love, for some
...Or so we believe, or so they perceive

Fallen

Lost in this world, I wonder where to turn
With nothing to lose and so many bridges I've burned

Clouds drift slowly across the full moon up above
In a starless sky on this night of doom without love
Down below resides me with a dagger clutched in my palm

Like an exploding pipe bomb granting a desired sense of calm
The illuminated blade shines the way to the hilltop up ahead
But my vision starts to fade and I see nothing but red
I close my eyes and drop to the ground
Crying out in anguish but not a damn soul is around

"The path I have chosen feels like it was chosen for me"
What else can I say? What else can I say?
There's nothing left to say on the ground that I lay

Nothing left to say on this earth which I lay..

Eternal Cycle

Deep in my eyes
Everyone has demised
Typhoon and kind soul
Fanged triple-bowl
Knife and self-torture
Staggering blood from punctured hole
Wonder if resurrected
Live forever breathing unknown
'Cause I'll never die
So bloody and high
As they pay up for the fine
Stab wound reply
Police stand-up line
Infinity lacked define
Cataclysmic demise
In the sky falling before thy eye
Shooting star
Scarred
Alive
So long dear lie...
The cycle has ended
Begun

Goodbye Forever

Goodbye my friend
I'm going away and I'm never coming back
Just thought I'd let you know

in case you ever came looking for me

I wish you luck in your life
I wish you luck with school
I wish you luck in this world,
this cold cruel heartless world

Goodbye my friend
I'm going away and I ain't ever coming back

Goodbye my friend, Goodbye forever..

The Death of All Life

I inhaled the fumes of a damned civilization
Of a parasitic species hell-bent on destructive creation
Transcending all other life, we were superior like a God
Or so we proclaimed and continued on with our song
We lied to ourselves that this day would never come
But now with nowhere to run and no place to hide
Everything's come to an end but at least I'm by your side

There were bombs and nukes, and smog pumped into the sky by the ton
And now never again will anyone feel the warmth of the sun
Never again will we bask in the light of the moon
Nevermore will we dream any dreams, only our doom
As I look up for the last time at the reddish orange sky
It just seems so fucking tragic like a tearless cry
The clouds begin to expand and collide, and yet, I have no need to ask why
Only kiss you goodbye as all life starts to die

Hold me close because this will be the last time you do
We won't ever again, it's such a shame but it's true
As the world begins to demolish and goes up in such pitiful flames
At least we're together on this dreadful, dying day
When everything once loved, feared or hated just fades away like a dream
Because it's the death of all life on this planet, this planet once green

("So it goes..")

Raindrops
(With an illustration from Jorge Santiago)

I'ma tell you a story about an adolescent I once knew
He was young and naïve without a shit of a clue
He believed he could conquer and dreamed of a better life
It was a life without pain as he walked in the rain
He walked down the edge of the street with his headset in hand
Listening to Q101 always took him to a far away land
As the raindrops fell onto the shades he sported as dark as his clothing
It distorted his vision and washed away any self-loathing

He was in his own world until arriving upon his destination
Where he saw a man with a knife at the train station
It all happened so fast, it was all such a blur
He fell to the ground and tried to cause a stir
He screamed out for help as the blade protruded from his side
They then left with his wallet and quarter gram as he died

As I'm kneeling by the train tracks with a spray can in my hand
I hear a long agonizing scream and sense a commotion
Off in the distance, a swift stabbing motion
I stop what I'm doing and run to the scene
Only to find a bloody dead body and it feels like a dream
In a state of panic, I look again upon the recognizable face
It's such a pity, the human race

Five years down the road, I sit in the back of a squad car
And I'm writing a letter to an old (deceased) friend afar
I have so many questions that can never be answered
Like, just how sacred is life when it can be taken so easily?
And is loss of innocence permanent like a rock smashed into debris?
Will it ever make sense? Will I ever understand?
And are questions like this just the price I must pay as a thinking man?
With no time to waste, I pull my forty-four
And three minutes later, I exit out the driver-seat door

A terrible thunderstorm but it's quite okay
I like it this way, walking in the rain
With so much in this world that could've been mine
And so much I've lost, it could never all fit in a short little rhyme
So many chances I missed with the excuse that it just wasn't my time
But what goes around comes around (at least that's what they say)
Still some things just linger like scars and never go away

Acknowledgements

Thanks to everyone who backed As the Moonlight Shines on Kickstarter! This book wouldn't exist without you guys.

Dayna Garcia

Deirdre Roberts

Lalinda De La Fuente

Barbara Ann Siemens

George Gant

Steve Aultz

Priscilla Boyd

Lindsay Moore

"Ron Paul (Fuck Yeah!)"

Tim Rossi

Ryan F. Skelly

Lara Ulanowski

Courtny Bindewald

Richard Pace

Hanna Marie

Drena Jo

Mark-Anthony Cardenas

Diane Rockell

Brad Boykin

Bookie's | New & Used Books

Monica Bailey

Ed Kolkebeck

Grant Williams

Kendra Reinshagen

Destinee Jones

Chloe Handle

Dan Dougherty

"Pistol Pete"

Donna L. Ulanowski

Meredith Ward

Jamie Rotante

David Pepose

Frank Gogol

Alex Stritar

Robert Gill

Special thanks to **Jorge Santiago** for the amazing cover art, the Raindrops illustration and the front and back cover design on this book. Thanks to **David Pepose** and **Action Lab Entertainment** for the graphic novel Spencer & Locke that put Jorge Santiago on my radar. Thanks to **Kristin Palmer** for the awesome watercolor illustration for Garlic Soup for the Soul. Thanks to **Kellie Lachata** who took the coffee shop photos of me that I used for the Kickstarter campaign. She also read and critiqued a lot of my poetry back in the day. Thanks to my friends **Ed Kolkebeck**, **Barbara Ann Siemens** and **Deirdre Roberts** for moral support and encouragement during my Kickstarter campaign. Thanks to **Dan Dougherty** for his help and advice with self-publishing and running a Kickstarter campaign. And thanks to **the good folks at Kickstarter** who gave me the crowdfunding platform I needed to make this book a reality!

Finally, an extra special thanks to **Steve Aultz**. He guided and mentored me through my many years of writing poetry. This book just wouldn't exist without him.